The Legends of Nod

The Legends of Nod

Book I

The Dragons of Nod

Being the first volume in the first saga
The Sword of Libran

A story from
The Epic of Prince Joryn

by

Glenn Slade Clark, Jr.

2019

The Legends of Nod, Book I:
The Dragons of Nod

This novelette was originally published as
The Legends of Nod #1 "The Dragons of Nod."

This edition has been revised and expanded by the author.

Cover art by Molly Fine.

ISBN-10: 1-61815-111-8
ISBN-13: 978-1-61815-111-7

For my inner child
and for yours.

CONTENTS

Dramatis Personae

<u>Charger</u> – Unicorn male from the Field of Crystal, age 300 years; son of Sir Illium and Lady Norlan; royal steed of Prince Kail

<u>Lord Galen</u> – Human male from the Imperial colony of the Whispering Plains, age nineteen years; son of Lord Pleidies and Lady Galendria; Lord of Ruby Point; paramour of Prince Joryn

<u>Sir Illium</u> – Unicorn male from the Golden Field, age 1,000 years; son of Ryjan and Maladine; husband of Lady Norlan; father of Charger; knight of the Order of the Golden Field; royal steed of Prince Joryn

Prince Joryn – Human male from the Kingdom of Nod, age twenty years; youngest son of Emperor Sapros and the Unnamed Empress; younger brother of Prince Kail, youngest half-brother of Prince Repteré, Princess Willowyll, Prince Dakarai, Princess Hero, Prince Mwana, Princess Adaeze, Prince Dorago, Princess Enjinia, Prince Vail, and Princess Lily; paramour of Lord Galen

Kabed – Human male from the kingdom of Deluvia, age twenty-four years; tech wizard; Imperial head of science for Emperor Sapros

Prince Kail – Human male from the Kingdom of Nod, age thirty-five years; eldest son of Emperor Sapros and the Unnamed Empress; older brother of Prince Joryn, eldest half-brother of Prince Repteré, Princess Willowyll, Prince Dakarai, Princess Hero, Prince Mwana, Princess Adaeze, Prince Dorago, Princess Enjinia, Prince Vail, and Princess Lily; husband of Princess Maressah; heir apparent to the thrones of both the Kingdom of Nod and the Empire of Nod; member of Emperor Sapros' Advisory Council

Governor Sunjac – Human male from the city of Bluepearl, age sixty-five years; son of Governor Bonak and Lady Perriella; governor of the city of Bluepearl

General Zaur – Dragon male from the city of Din, age 5,073 years; general of the Royal Army of Dragons in the service of Queen Shaakkanaah

The Legends of Nod

Book I

The Dragons of Nod

CHAPTER 1:

THE UNICORN'S NEW LEGS

J ORYN PERCHED ON A LEDGE ON THE CLIFFSIDE BELOW the great palace, staring at the Celestine Sea. He watched the golden sun appear to rise out of the waters, marking the birth of a new day. It seemed strange to him that, only hours before, he had thought time would have to stand still forever. If the gods were just, the tragic events that now seemed inevitable could not actually be allowed to come to pass. A tear escaped his eye, as he wondered what dark news the day would bring.

His dearest friend had been injured in a battle that neither of them had foreseen. Joryn hadn't spoken of the battle to anyone since reporting that it had happened and that it had been the cause of Illium's inescapably mortal wounds.

He hadn't bothered with the details. He only wanted Illium to pull through.

A shadow was cast from behind him, as his mind wandered back to the present. The young prince did not even bother to turn. Somehow, he recognized the presence behind the shadow; the calm demeanor and genuine concern. "I know. I should be attending to my princely duties."

"Concern for your people is the greatest of your princely duties, I would say, Little Brother. Better to find you staring at the ocean with a tear in your eye than to find you drowning your sorrows in some tavern and shaming us all."

Joryn considered the words of his older brother. If he had not come to drag him to some duty, he had only bothered to seek him out for one reason. There was news of Illium. How Joryn both dreaded and yearned for the knowledge of his friend's fate. "They say the sea is endless, much as a unicorn's life is meant to be." A lump formed in his throat.

"Which is why I've come," Kail said.

Joryn turned slowly to face his oldest brother. "Has it happened?" He let out a breath, deeply pained, forcing himself to keep breathing under the weight of his grief. "Is he gone?"

Kail laughed. "No. He's come through."

Joryn was on his feet and beaming with the thrill of the news in an instant, gripping his brother. "Kabed is a genius! How did he do it? There was hardly anything left to work with!"

A careful look came over the older prince. "You'll have to come and see for yourself. Illium will want to see you too." He paused. "I should warn you, it's not what you might expect. Be prepared for a shock, but Illium is alive."

Concerned, Joryn asked, "Is it bad?"

"No. Just … a change."

Puzzled, Joryn looked away from his brother and made to climb the wall back up to the palace. "I must go to him."

"Wouldn't it be safer to follow the winding path?"

Joryn paused and looked at the path, then to the sheer cliffside before him, as he started to pull himself upwards.

"Safer, yes. But this is much faster, and my heart can't take the wait."

Prince Kail laughed. "Then I suppose I'll join you." The older man threw his cape full behind him and began ascending the cliff with his brother.

The two brothers entered Kabed's workshop breathlessly and were greeted not by the scientist himself but by the centaur Dorran Equus, an ambassador to the Imperial court representing the nomadic Caluman Tribe. "My lords," he took in the sight of them, fresh from their hurried climb, "you're filthy."

The brothers laughed at their friend's wry assessment, and Joryn asked urgently, "Equus, where's Illium?"

The centaur chuckled at the worry on the young man's face. "Easy, Prince Joryn. Illium is fine. Kabed just wanted to see him test his legs." Joryn regarded the centaur fearfully, and the creature laughed some more. "Stop worrying, my prince. I assure you, he's fine. I've been checking in by the hour all night. You know what friends we are."

"Thank you, Equus. I would have done the same myself, but I had my 'princely duties.' "

"No need to explain. You've done more than enough already. And your princely duties are important."

" 'More than enough.' " Joryn made a face. "He wouldn't have even *come* so near to death if not for me."

Equus folded his arms and earnestly asked his young friend, "Was it because of *you* that he was torn to pieces, or was it because of the creature who attacked you?"

Joryn looked down at the floor. "I know what you're trying to do, Equus. I know you're right." He met the centaur's gaze. "But I still feel responsible. It was *my* idea to go out so far. When that monster attacked us, I should have been able to defeat him, but his claws were just too powerful."

Prince Kail interrupted, "You've said nothing of the battle before now other than that you were bested and had to drag your steed home in pieces. What sort of monster was this that attacked you? What happened?"

A loud, agonized breath escaped the young prince as he resolved to tell the tale. "It was horrible, Kail. The thing itself was a nightmare. Crab-like and gigantic, three times the size of a normal man. It spoke the tongue of Nod, but looked incapable of words, though in its monstrous demeanor, still I saw some semblance of humanity in its build. It had no weapons other than its pincers. But they were enormous. They snapped both of my swords in two."

"I've never heard of such a creature," Equus offered, mystified. "Where do you suppose it came from?"

"He said his name was Warclaw; that he was the son of Cancerelle."

"Ah," Equus pondered that. "The son of a goddess, no less." He laughed derisively. "And who did he say his father was?"

"He didn't." Joryn shook his head. "I know it seems unlikely, Equus, but after I fought this creature I had no reason to doubt that he was, in fact, the son of Cancerelle. Crustaceans have always been her servants, have they not?"

A new voice broke into the conversation, "So you *do* pay attention to some of Parakletos' lessons." The new arrival was Kabed, the young man from the mysterious, isolated kingdom of Deluvia, who had served in the palace as Head of Science since Prince Joryn had spoken up for him five years before.

"Kabed! Where is Illium?"

"I am here, my young prince," came the voice of Illium, as he trotted through the door. He whinnied happily, rising up on his new hind legs and showing off for his prince.

"By the gods!" Joryn laughed, as he regarded the ancient unicorn. "You really are alive!"

"What's this?" the eldest prince said, as he mussed his brother's hair. "Prince Joryn smiling? Could it be that he's back to his usual self at last?" He regarded Kabed. "You really do work miracles. Two cures with one operation." He studied his brother. "What do you think?"

Joryn stared at the new Illium. "How is it possible? Will the wonders of Deluvian science never cease?" He spoke to the unicorn. "You look like a war horse, but your armor has become your very body."

The unicorn stood proudly. "The Deluvian has fitted me with cybernetic parts to replace those lost in the battle with Warclaw. My chest and all four of my legs have been replaced. The greatest challenge of course was saving my heart. I doubt even the Deluvians could replicate its functions if it had to be replaced, but Kabed managed to keep it beating long enough to fit it into the functions of my new body."

"Well, I had to." Kabed laughed as he patted the unicorn on the neck. "After a thousand years in Nod, I don't think the sky would stay up without you."

Everyone laughed at this.

"But how did you manage this so quickly, Kabed?" Joryn went to Illium and stroked his mane, smiling up at him.

"As it turns out, I had already been working on a mechanical unicorn to meet the needs of your father. I thought perhaps it would please him to be the only man in Nod to command an army of *Deluvian* unicorns. I intended them to be war machines, to be used in defense of the kingdom in these strange times. I had enough of one built that it was only a matter of working what remained of Illium into its shell and, of course, getting the whole thing symbiotic."

Joryn beamed. "Bless you, Kabed."

Another unicorn pushed the door to Kabed's workshop open with his horn. This was Charger, Illium's much younger son and the official steed of Prince Kail. "Father," he said to Illium, quietly marveling at the method of his survival, "it's good to see you up and around." Having last seen his father so close to death, he found himself fighting the urge to forget his present task, to give voice to the storm of worry and relief that roiled within his heart at the sight of his father, alive and well and forever transformed. But unicorns were known to be a people of few words. He looked to the men in the room. "Forgive me for being short, but the ambassadors from the Whispering Plains are about to depart."

"Oh, no!" Joryn breathed. "Galen!"

"I understand," Illium said. "Let's go." He indicated with a gesture of his head that the young prince should mount up.

"But you're ..."

"Better than new. Climb on and let's go, or you may not have a chance to say your goodbyes."

Reluctantly, Joryn leaped up onto the bionic unicorn and allowed himself to be carried swiftly from the workshop.

"Well?" Charger asked of his own appointed rider.

Prince Kail laughed. "You may not have iron legs, Charger, but you're still the only unicorn for me." He leapt onto the creature's back and turned to Kabed. "Coming?"

"Oh ... yeah. I just have to clean up and ..."

"Get on, Kabed!" The prince laughed as he held out his hand.

"You're the prince." Kabed took the offered hand and mounted Charger, sitting behind Prince Kail, and the three of them made their way to the landing terrace.

Being a centaur, Dorran Equus watched them go, then said to them, sure that no one would hear, "I think I'll stay behind and eat. What? No protest? Well then, it's settled," and he made his way to the workshop's little kitchen to eat as much of Kabed's snack food as he could.

Chapter 2:

The Dragons Attack

THE TWO PRINCES ARRIVED WITH THEIR STEEDS TOO late for Joryn to offer Galen a heartfelt farewell. It was all pomp and ceremony now. Joryn's other five older brothers were already in position behind their father, as were his five older sisters.

King Sapros, red-faced with an inner rage that was all too often set loose on his subordinates, did his best to remain calm. "Take your places, while I still *bother* to reserve them for you."

As the two princes dismounted their steeds, the king gave Illium a distasteful once-over.

Kabed bowed and made his way to the sidelines.

The unicorn simply snorted in the king's direction and trotted along with Charger to the edge of the great landing platform, behind the humans and out of their way.

To his eldest son, now standing at his right side, the king said, "So nice of you to join us at last."

Kail whispered, "We were seeing to Illium. I apologize for the delay. He was testing out his new legs."

"The fate of some *unicorn* is nothing compared to your duty as heir to the throne of Imperial Nod. Do not let *animals* command your time. Command theirs instead."

"I hear you, Father."

"Clever choice of words," the king muttered, trying to keep his own words below the detection of their visitors from the Plains. "They neither agree with nor contest what I say."

"Why should I contest the words of my king and father?"

The king rolled his eyes, his temper cooling much to his own annoyance. He knew what Kail was doing. It was what he always did. He was diffusing the situation, placating him without ever agreeing with him. The most irritating thing about this skill of his eldest son's was how effectively he wielded it.

The dignitaries from the Whispering Plains marched onto the platform, flanking Lord Pleidies and his son Galen. Perhaps Joryn alone was aware how disgruntled Galen was by the formality of the farewell ceremony, having been required by his father to wear a sword at his side, rather than the pistols he was accustomed to.

Standing trapped by his *own* prison of formality, between Willowyll, his oldest sister, and Vail, the youngest of his older brothers, Joryn locked eyes with Galen and found them as desperate for escape as were his own. Galen smiled slightly in his direction, and Joryn nodded his acknowledgement, only to hear the disapproving sigh of his sister wordlessly reminding him not to break form.

Joryn did as was expected of him, as did Galen, and it was a torture to both of them. Lord Pleidies and his retinue had been invited to the Imperial palace, at Joryn's urging, in order to attend Charger's lavish tricentennial birthday celebration. Of course, the real reason Joryn had urged his unicorn friends to extend the invitation was so that he could see Galen again. The festivities had come and gone three days ago, and those three days with Galen had seemed as no time at all to the young lovers.

Joryn wished they could run away from all of the relentless grandeur and formality of their courtly lives; that they could be open about their love for one another without worrying about the political implications that would inevitably follow such an acknowledgment.

They had been hiding the true nature of their relationship from their families and friends for nearly a year, hoping to avoid the inevitable politicization of what they had found in each other's arms. This love was theirs, and theirs alone. It was sacred to them, and they wanted to keep it that way for as long as they possibly could.

Lord Pleidies bowed before King Sapros. Galen and the dignitaries followed his lead. "We offer our most humble thanks to Your Majesty, King Sapros, emperor of the kingdoms of Nod, for your limitless generosity and hospitality. We will strive to live up to your example if ever you are a visitor in the Whispering Plains."

King Sapros nodded. "May the gods bless your journey home, Lord Pleidies."

The ramp on the great flying vessel behind the Plains people descended then, and the dignitaries began to file up onto the ship.

An ear-shattering roar caused everyone to jump at that very moment, and the people gathered on the landing terrace looked to the sky with horror.

The alarm began wailing from the palace watchtower, and the king growled in anger.

"Dragons!" Prince Vail was the first to break formation, drawing his sword. "We must fight!"

"Put that sword away, you melodramatic idiot!" The king gritted his teeth, then bellowed, "Guards to battle stations! Defend the palace!"

The dragons took position in the sky and, on the command of their leader, lashed out at the palace with flame from their throats.

The guards ran out and began leading people to cover.

Joryn found a way to lose himself in the hysterical crowd and get to Illium and Charger, who stood watching, seemingly without fear.

Tianna, the nineteen-year-old priestess of Libran, made her way quietly over to them as well. "What's this all about," she asked Illium, never taking her eyes from the sky.

Still watching the sky with dread himself, Illium answered her, "This has been expected for some time now. They come once every three kings, though no one ever knows the year they will choose. Their leader," Illium nodded in the head dragon's direction, "is General Zaur. He has been at the head of the last four such attacks."

"What do they intend to do?" she asked. "What is the purpose?"

"They test us," the unicorn answered. "They want to expand their territory. Whatever the reason, our kings have perpetually failed to hold them off. Within the month, I'd say, the dragons will advance, and no fewer than ten cities will be laid waste."

Prince Joryn was incensed. "If we knew this was coming …"

"Why didn't your father tell you?" Illium smiled at the young man with his eyes.

"I am his youngest and least valuable son. He tells me nothing." Joryn thought back on the many history lessons he had received from his venerable mentor Parakletos, and he realized that his father had not been the only one who had been keeping this inevitability a secret. He thought to himself, *Probably just one more thing my father has forbidden to be spoken in the Empire ... like Mother's name.*

"Oh," Tianna said, breaking his solemn introspection, "you're far from the least valuable, Joryn. I've seen omens, recently."

Joryn met her eyes. "And I have seen defeat. I'm the prince who nearly got the oldest unicorn in Nod killed yesterday, if you'll recall."

Kabed ran up to the group then. "My prince, Priestess, I *have* to get you both to safety. The dragons are diving."

They all looked to the sky and saw the dragons begin to descend. Joryn found Galen and Lord Pleidies in the crowd, not entering their craft for fear of it being blasted out of the air by the malevolence of the dragon breath that so relentlessly burned all in its path.

"We have to get the Plains people to safety too," Joryn insisted. "Galen and his father are still out there right in the middle of it all."

"I agree," offered Kabed. "But my first duty is to you." He looked to Tianna.

Just then they heard Galen cry out.

Joryn looked on in horror as the young man drew his sword.

Lord Pleidies whacked the dragon, who flapped his great wings above them, with his scepter, only to be knocked back like a mere insect by the untroubled effort of a single dragon talon.

The great beast reached out to grab the young man, and Galen slashed its claws with his sword, spilling enough blood to drown a child, yet still not causing the dragon more harm than a fleeting itch.

Joryn was stricken silent with fear, knowing there was nothing that he could do to stop what was about to happen.

The guards ran on to the scene, shooting at the creature with the Deluvian light guns that Kabed had introduced them to.

The dragon angrily blew flames in their direction, reducing them instantly to ash and charred metal.

Galen swung again at the creature, and it sneered at him, amused and disgusted all at once, as it simply grabbed him, sword and all, in its black talons.

The young man's wide and horrified eyes found Joryn and silently screamed out for salvation.

"Galen!" Joryn drew his own sword at last and ran towards the dragon, still knowing in his heart there was nothing he could do, but willing to die trying nonetheless.

"Joryn, no! It's too late! That dragon won't hesitate to incinerate you!" Kabed ran after the young prince and took hold of his shoulders, stopping him in his tracks.

Both of them watched helplessly then, as Galen was spirited away into the sky.

Dragon fire and Deluvian light rays filled the air, as General Zaur ordered a retreat. The dragons vanished into the distance just as quickly as they had arrived.

His face blackened by the smoke that rose from fallen soldiers and debris, Joryn ran to the king, who was helping Lord Pleidies to stand. "Father!" Tears streamed down Prince Joryn's face, as he met his father's furious stare.

"My son!" Pleidies was sobbing, as the king held him up. "They took my only son!"

Prince Kail came to stand beside the king. "We'll get him back. I assure you the throne will act quickly and de—"

"*No!*" The king lashed out at his oldest son, knocking him to the ground with a powerful arm. "There is *nothing* we can do! Nothing. Galen is lost to us, and the dragons will once again push their boundaries closer to the heart of Nod."

"No …" Pleidies offered this only as a whisper, seeming to lose his very heart within the word.

King Sapros glared at Kabed, as he approached the scene. "You! I should have your head for this!"

"My king?"

Sapros rushed at Kabed and shoved him to the ground forcefully.

Joryn protested, "Father! Kabed has done nothing wrong! We were better defended because of the technology that he—"

"*Silence!*" The king swung at Joryn, but the prince avoided the blow. "You pathetic *infant!* How dare you contest me at a time like this!"

"But, Father, you're—"

"Joryn," came the voice of Kail, once again rising to stand beside his father. He gave his brother an urgent look. "Do not forget your place." He motioned his head towards their father.

Joryn hung his head, submitting more to his brother's wisdom than to their father's insanity. The king then struck him in the face, and Joryn fell obediently to the ground.

Resuming his attack on Kabed, the king said, "You were to have those Unitrons *ready* for this! You promised me an army riding to our defense on mechanical unicorns, fully equipped with Deluvian light weaponry and made of Deluvian steel! And what do I find instead?" He pointed to Illium in the distance. "You *wasted* the prototype on *that*! I should have you put to death!"

"Father," Joryn spoke from the ground, where he sat massaging his jaw, "Kabed *saved* Illium's life! The prototype was not wasted at all."

The king drew his sword and turned on his youngest son. *"Damn you to the nine hells of the centaurs, boy, I swear by the throne I'll send you to the gods myself this instant!"*

Moving subtly in the path of his father's sword, Prince Kail offered heatedly, "Father, you have my support in punishing Kabed for this outrageous use of our resources."

Nonplussed, King Sapros opened and closed his mouth, trying to find the words, then, "... I do?"

"Absolutely," Kail went on. "If he hadn't used the prototype in the way he had, if he'd not saved Illium, a unicorn who hasn't even *spoken* to you in over twenty years, he would have been able to spend the night finishing the Unitron. The hopeless battle that we just endured would have been its test. We would still have lost, of course, but we might have taken some of those dragons down with us. And we would know the capabilities of the Unitron and be able to start work immediately on the construction of more."

"Precisely!" The king seemed to forget that he had been on the verge of murdering his youngest son, but he still did not sheathe his sword. He turned to Kabed, giving the young scientist a hateful once-over. "We should never have let Joryn talk us into this," he said to Kail. "Letting a Deluvian runaway work in the palace. Giving him so much power. Let's waste no more time in ending the mistake."

"Yes," Kail said, putting a hand on his father's shoulder in camaraderie, subtly keeping the man from raising his sword. "He should be punished, so that he will remember that there are consequences for displeasing the king. Kabed is too valuable an asset for us to let him forget his place in this palace."

Quietly bewildered, but yielding to his son's reason, the king looked at Kabed appraisingly. "This is true."

"I would be honored," Kail offered with a sneer of visible contempt at the Deluvian, "to take the burden of his punishment from your shoulders. You have a war on your hands now. You shouldn't be troubled by this. I look forward to finding a suitable punishment on my own."

The king nodded, highly satisfied by the words of his heir. "Very well then." He looked intensely into Kail's blue eyes. "See that he *never* forgets his place again." Without another word, the king stormed back into the palace.

When their father was out of earshot, Joryn rose and challenged his brother. "How can you take *his* side? He's insane! He was going to *kill* us!"

"Yet he did not." Kail smiled at his brother and winked at the terrified Kabed with a laugh. He explained to Joryn, "Those who excel the most at politics tend to be the ones with little to no taste for the game itself. They do it to take care of the people they care for, because they know the winner of any such match has determined who gets what when." He removed his most prized ring from his finger and tossed it to

Kabed. "Check it for cracks, will you? And consider yourself duly punished."

Kabed, understanding, laughed with dawning relief. "Right away, Prince Kail."

Kail shook a finger in mock condemnation. "And let that be a lesson to you."

When Kabed had gone, Kail said to his brother, "You need to learn how to say what needs to be said without rousing the anger in your opponents, Little Brother."

Joryn looked to the sky. "Maybe such skills will come easier to me when I'm an old, married man like you."

"Thirty-five is not old."

"And twenty is not an *infant*. When will Father ever see me as a man?"

Kail put a hand on his brother's shoulder and met his eyes. "When you no longer need him to."

Both brothers looked to the sky, wondering what was to become of Galen.

"For now," Kail said, "take comfort in the fact that *I* know the man you have become. Which is why I expect you'll be in trouble again very soon for what you're planning."

"How did you know?"

"I can tell how strongly you feel for Galen. If it were Maressah who'd been taken, I'd be forming a plan as well. Just be careful. Remember that you'll do him no good if all you manage to do is get yourself killed. The key ingredient to any good plan is patience."

Joryn wondered if Kail actually *could* tell how strongly he felt for Galen, but still he remained silent on the matter, thinking to himself that patience was not always a virtue, and that every moment he spent forming a solid plan might be the very moment he would need back later, to save Galen's life.

The brothers stood there in silence for what seemed a very long time, watching the terrible sky.

CHAPTER 3:

JORYN SETS OUT

T HAT NIGHT, AS THE PALACE SLEPT, PRINCE Joryn repelled down the mountainside on a sturdy rope, hoping to escape the notice of any who might ask where he was going. He was adorned all in black, including a hooded cloak to blend in with the night. He had at his side the same sword he had carried with him to bid farewell to the Plains dignitaries earlier that day, and over his shoulder he carried a satchel, stuffed with what little food he had managed to sneak from the kitchen and changes of clothes for the journey ahead. He knew he was ill-prepared, but his plan to cross the Empire on foot left him little choice but to take what he could carry and hope to make it to a town and resupply before he starved to death. Indeed, the main reason Joryn had chosen to depart in stealth was to avoid anyone more sensible talking him out of this mad quest.

When he reached the bottom, Joryn dusted himself off and looked up at the rope, which hung by an iron hook from his bedroom window, and he decided to leave it there. His father would learn of his absence regardless. Better to let him know it had been Joryn's own will that took him from the palace.

Joryn surveyed his surroundings, trying to determine which way was east. He instinctually wanted to avoid the Dark Forest, and he began to make his way in accordance with that desire.

"You'll never get there in time, if you go in that direction; and on foot no less."

Joryn spun around, startled. He lowered his hood and smiled with relief when he saw who had found him out. "Illium! What brings you out so late?"

"My knowledge of you, of course," the unicorn answered.

Joryn laughed lightly, then said with a stern grin, "Well, you can't come with me, old friend. Not this time. It's too dangerous, and I'll surely incur my father's wrath. Besides, you've been injured. I won't have you …"

The unicorn trotted towards him, as Joryn's words trailed off. "You cannot leave me behind simply because of what happened the last time. I'm better than new. And I will not let you go through the Dark Forest alone." Illium's eyes twinkled with their own kind of smile as he spoke. "For that is the fastest way, my prince; and my new legs will take us there even faster. There is no time to spare if we are to try and save the border lands and rescue young Galen."

Joryn sighed, as he resigned himself. "All right, Illium. I confess. You know me well." He walked over and pulled himself up onto the unicorn's back. "But even I know when I'm being *too* idealistic. Though my heart desires it, there is nothing that the two of us can do to save the cities of the border lands."

"One never knows," offered the unicorn, as his mechanical legs began to carry them straight into the Dark Forest. "Sometimes all it takes is *being* there."

CHAPTER 4:

BLUEPEARL'S FATE

THE TWO FRIENDS TRAVELED FOR WEEKS WITH little trouble at all. They stopped in towns to buy food and at rivers to rest and drink. Joryn had not hesitated upon first daybreak to pack away his black ensemble for his more customary colors. He still preferred his black boots, which were the perfect contrast to his usual light-colored pants and shirts. As for vests, he had only worn shades of blue since the day Galen had adoringly pointed out that blue brought out the color of his eyes. And Joryn was seldom ever seen that his form was not framed with a beautiful red cape.

In spite of Joryn dressing in this way, they made an effort not to be recognized, though Illium did draw a great deal of attention. Not only was it uncommon for just anyone to be allowed to ride a unicorn, but a *bionic* unicorn was absolutely unheard of in all of Nod. When strangers asked, Joryn told them only of Illium's accident and how a Deluvian scientist had saved his life. He said nothing specific and was fortunate that word of Illium's transformation had not yet left the palace.

As for Joryn's polished, princely clothing, weeks of travel, without taking the time to stop and launder, saw to it that it did not appear so regal as when they had first set out. This only added to the prince's anonymity, as the two friends pressed on.

It would normally have taken six weeks to reach the eastern borders of Emperor Sapros' realm on horseback, but with the help of Illium's untiring legs, the pair made the journey in only three weeks and five days. They made their way into a glistening city called Bluepearl (having been named for a treasure acquired for them by an ancient hero, before the days of the human empire), and had not been there long enough even for the people to marvel at Illium before the trouble began.

People were running from shops and taverns, frantic, as if the city had been breached by an invading army.

Joryn asked a man as they passed, "What's the trouble here, sir?"

"The watchtower spotted dragons in the air, headed in our direction. Word is they incinerated Brookdale yesterday. We've heard they even attacked the Royal Palace of King Sapros himself, less than a month ago. You chose a poor time to pay a visit, stranger."

The man suddenly seemed to notice Illium.

"Thank you, sir," Joryn replied blankly, as Illium moved ahead, leaving the man to stare after them in wonder.

"What do you intend to do?" Illium asked.

Joryn stared off to the horizon, which was jagged and red where the titanic Mountains of Flame met the clouds in the distance. "Whatever I must. We still have a long way to go before we reach the dragons' city in the mountains. If we make a stand here, we'll be killed."

"Your voice does not sound firm."

"That's because," the prince continued, "if we do nothing, the people of this city will be killed, along with all the work of their ancestors. And I will know that we did nothing; that we abandoned them."

Illium nodded somberly. "Such are the decisions that are made by kings."

"Then for once I feel sorry for my father." Tears welled up silently in Joryn's eyes, as he allowed Illium to continue passing through the doomed city of Bluepearl.

The dragons arrived just as Illium reached the city's eastern border.

Joryn pulled back gently on Illium's mane, signaling the unicorn to stop. The young prince stared out ahead of them, as the people began to scream out in terror. The city behind him trembled beneath the powerful roar of the dragons. Joryn closed his eyes and tried to breathe through the moment, as he fought a fierce battle within himself, unsure which of his passions would claim victory over his troubled heart.

"If I just run for a moment, we'll leave all this behind us," Illium offered; an odd tone in his voice.

The prince slowed his breathing, making his decision. "I can't do it, Illium." Joryn opened his eyes. "I know we'll be killed here for even trying, but I can't live knowing that I abandoned every soul in Bluepearl to rescue only one. Besides, we'd likely be killed by the dragons later on just the same." He nudged the unicorn gently. "To the center of the city, Illium!"

The unicorn turned and reared up, whinnying excitedly, then launched into an amazing sprint to the middle of Bluepearl, where the dragons were taking formation in the sky.

Prince Joryn drew his sword and held it aloft, as Illium came to a halt and reared up once more, the white horn of his head suddenly shining gold, in keeping with the unicorn's tremendous spirit of hope.

The few people who had not the courage or desire to run gathered in the shadows of the buildings and watched in astonishment.

"General Zaur!" Joryn addressed the dragon leader boldly. "I request parley on behalf of Bluepearl and of the emperor, Sapros!"

Flame licked the outside of several of the dragons' mouths, as the general spoke in a powerful voice, through disdainful laughter. "Hold your fire and your positions." He swooped down, closer to the ground, covering the square with his tremendous shadow. He took in the sight of Prince Joryn and his unusual steed. "Who are *you* to request parley with the Dragons of Nod?"

It was only the rush of adrenaline that kept the prince's heart from failing within him. "I am Prince Joryn, son of Sapros our emperor."

"*Your* emperor, boy. He is no more than an insect to us."

"Nevertheless, he is *our* emperor, and I am here on his behalf to come to some agreement."

"If you mean to discuss the terms of your surrender," Zaur suggested, "*our* leader is not interested. We were sent to ruin this city. The order was quite plain."

Panic began to enter the young man's voice. "But ... *why?* Why are the dragons doing this?"

More laughter erupted from the great, red-scaled dragon, as he answered succinctly, "Why not?"

Joryn watched the smoke roiling up into the sky from the sides of the dragon's snout, as the general studied him. He forced himself to remain outwardly stalwart, in spite of the unspoken threat. "Because, the people of our realm have not done anything to merit this. We've lived in peace for generations."

Zaur considered. "You seem earnest, young princeling, so I'll indulge you this question. The dragons have a longstanding tradition of razing your cities. We were here *millions* of years before humanity. All of Nod belonged to us. Your people usurped what was ours, laying claim to lands that were never theirs to claim. That is why, every three human kings, we return to claim a little bit more of what is rightfully ours.

"You of course have the right to surrender the entire realm to us now, and your people will only be enslaved. However, the cities will still be destroyed."

An old man came out from the shadows and raised a fist to the air. "Better to die now than live as slaves!"

The other Bluepearlians shouted their agreement.

Joryn hushed them with an urgent wave of his hand. "My father would never do that, and neither can I. Is there no way we can come to a truce? After all, none have ever found the ends of Nod. The land goes on and the skies are forever. With all that room to our two societies, there must be some way to make peace over something so small in comparison as the territory of an empire."

The dragon's eyes narrowed, and his army roared impatiently above him. "And what if I simply burn you where you stand? *That* is what I have come here to do; not to listen to some *human* whine about peace."

Joryn shook his head sadly. "Then you fail to surprise me. It is the very thing that I expected of you. I know that there is nothing to be done here, if you will not consider peace. I *will* die. But I will shed the blood of many dragons before I do, though my sword is but a needle against your scales, because, in the end, I cannot give up hope. Stranger things have happened than a few humans and a unicorn winning the day over an army of dragons." He readied his sword, and, to his surprise, several compartments on Illium's hips and shoulders opened up, revealing Deluvian light guns aimed right at the dragon's heart. "So, if that is your decision …"

The dragon laughed thunderously at this. The ground trembled with every guffaw. When he caught his breath, he lowered his head to look right into Joryn's eyes. "Such courage! And we thought the trait had been bred out of your kind." He grinned ominously. "You will have your peace."

Joryn sighed audibly with relief.

The people murmured their astonishment.

The dragon raised his head and added, "For seven days!" He flew up higher, before speaking further, "I would not deprive our queen of the laughter you have given me this day. We dragons are a serious people and rarely take the time for such things. You have one week to make the journey and speak with her. But do not make the journey with any false hopes, young human. She will most *certainly* make a slave of you and resume her attacks on your father's cities." Zaur soared upwards then and flew off, leading his army back to the Mountains of Flame.

Joryn breathed out and let his face fall into Illium's mane.

The unicorn laughed with delight.

The old man, who had shouted out before, approached them then. "My prince, that was outstanding!"

Joryn looked over and took the man's proffered hand with a smile.

"I am Sunjac, governor of Bluepearl. Would you and Illium accept my hospitality before leaving on your journey? You will need food, water, and some rest before you brave the Wildlands."

"We would be honored," Joryn moaned with a tired laugh, and he slid exhaustedly off of Illium's back.

***

Sunjac's home was large, but cozy for the house of a governor. He proved to be a very well-educated man with walls in every room supporting shelves full of books. He spoke with Joryn and Illium well into the night, telling them all about the dragons and the cities beyond Bluepearl that had been razed seventy-nine years before, when his own father had still been governor of the city and he himself had yet to be born.

After a while, it was clearly time to let the young prince rest. Sunjac showed Illium to a very plush rug by the fireplace, where he could sleep (though Illium needed no such comforts and only accepted out of politeness), and he led Joryn to a room upstairs that looked out over the city when the shutters were open, letting in the moonlight and bathing the entire chamber in a soft, blue glow.

It took Joryn no time at all to fall asleep, after the day he had just seen through. It was the sleep of the righteous; earned only by those who have put their virtue to the test of fire and emerged just as faithful as they had dared to hope they would. It was a sleep of perfect peace. A sleep without dreams.

CHAPTER 5:

THIEVES IN THE NIGHT

LATE INTO THE NIGHT, A FEELING WOKE JORYN abruptly. He sat up with a start. "Who's there?" He peered into the shadows, trying to bat away the unreality of what must have been nothing more than a bad dream, trying to convince himself that was all that it had been. He slowly lay back down, but just before his head hit the pillow, he saw something. It was a figure standing where he'd laid his traveling clothes and sword. He sat up again. "Identify yourself."

A slithering sort of voice answered him from the darkness, as the figure moved forward. "Call out for help, and we will slay you here and now, rather than wait for you to arrive in the city of Din."

As the figure walked carefully past him, Joryn saw that while it was the size and mostly the build of a human, it was quite far removed from one as well. It had a long, powerful-looking tail and a pair of dragon-like wings on its back ... and it was carrying his sword and several other weapons that it appeared to have gathered from within the governor's house. Joryn began to say something, but the creature stopped him.

"I am not alone, young prince. Others may have knives to the throats of your friends even as we speak and will spare them only when they see I've gotten past you." The creature made its way cautiously to the great window, never taking his eyes off of the prince until he leapt into the air and was carried off by those leathery wings.

Joryn was left feeling utterly defeated.

After enough time had passed that he was sure the creatures had left the house, Joryn went to check on Illium and Sunjac, finding them unharmed but troubled by what they both had seen.

As the dawn broke in Bluepearl, the people compared notes. Very few had awakened during the invasion, and none of them had been disturbed by a sound; only a feeling. The strange creatures had gone to every home and shop in the entire city and stolen every weapon.

Bluepearl was defenseless.

"But why would they do such a thing?" Sunjac shook his head. "Our defenses were nothing against an army of dragons as it was."

"Were the dragons behind this?" another man asked. "How can you be sure?"

"Though I've never seen anything like them or heard of such creatures in any tale, those thieves were certainly some sort of cross between the species. And if they sided with us, they would not have taken our weapons."

Illium took this all in silently.

Joryn spoke up, sorrowfully, "I fear it is my doing." He met Sunjac's eyes. "The dragons could level Bluepearl easily, defended or not. But I am the one who must still journey through the Wildlands to get to their city within the week. They likely robbed the entire town to make sure I had no weapons at my side."

Sunjac nodded. "I agree. They fear you, I think. It may sound unheroic of me, but I must urge you to turn away from this quest. Return to the palace. There is nothing you can accomplish by setting out to the Wildlands unarmed. You will be set upon by some horror and killed like a helpless child among the wolves."

Illium surprised the crowd then by speaking directly to Sunjac, "In my time, I have seen many strange things. Sometimes a child can walk with the wolves. Sometimes, the wolves admire the child, rather than attack it."

"I do not question your wisdom, Illium. But I do take note of the word 'sometimes' in your argument." Sunjac shook his head. "Turn back, my prince. You cannot help us any more by dying."

Joryn looked away, towards the mountains. "It's more than that. I must go on."

"But, Prince Joryn …"

"My friend is a prisoner of the dragons, and I would lay down my life to save him." He met Sunjac's gaze once more and found nothing but admiration there. "It is true that I may die, but I might have died yesterday as well, when I asked General Zaur for parley. Bluepearl may fall because I fail, but it will not fall because I fail to try. And if I don't try, you will fall just the same. I *must* go on."

The prince took hold of the horn of Illium's saddle, and stopped before putting his foot in the stirrup, noticing the glorious red coloring of the seat that the unicorn now wore. He smiled, amused by his friend's uncharacteristic flair. "What is this? A new saddle?"

"A gift from Governor Sunjac," Illium answered, a warm smile in his eyes.

"My nephew is the finest saddler in Bluepearl," Sunjac offered proudly. "This saddle will give much greater comfort to both you and Illium, my prince. And, of course I will have your old saddle sent back to the palace. It was not my intention to claim Imperial property for myself. I wished only to thank you both, in what little way I could."

The prince beamed at the old man. "No, Governor. Please, keep the saddle, let your own horse wear a saddle that bears the Imperial seal, the saddle that carried us to your city, as a reminder of our friendship, in gratitude for the kindness you have shown us."

Overwhelmed by the gesture, Sunjac bowed. "My prince, thank you."

"Not at all, Governor. It is my thanks to *you*." The prince mounted his steed, and the unicorn began to move. Joryn turned back to Sunjac then, and Illium paused. "Do you have a communications monitor in your room?"

"Yes."

"Please contact my father, and tell him where I am and where I'm headed."

"Will he send help?" the governor asked hopefully.

Somberly, Joryn gazed at the mountains in the distance, knowing that his father would not. "Few men are either fool or genius enough to challenge the inevitable. If I were you, I would evacuate. Meanwhile, I will do what I can in Din."

As they rode away from Bluepearl, Illium's eyes twinkled with approval at the prince's words. The boy he had known so long had indeed become a man.

CHAPTER 6:

WHEN ALL SEEMS LOST

J ORYN AND ILLIUM TRAVELED THE DESOLATE Wildlands
for three days without incident. They passed the ruins of
several former settlements that had been destroyed by
invasions past. The landscape was dreary. The closer they
came to the great red mountains, the less they saw of any
vegetation, and there was no shade at all, save for the quickly
passing clouds.

They made their way into the Broken Desert, where fault lines had opened and never reclosed. The pathways were narrow, sometimes flanked on each side by chasms of incredible depth. Illium trod carefully.

It was during this leg of their journey that trouble at last came their way. Illium stopped, and both he and Joryn shielded their eyes as an intense, shimmering light appeared before them on the narrow path. The light became a shape, and the shape became a solid creature. It was Warclaw, the very villain who had nearly killed Illium weeks before.

The great crab-like creature laughed at the sight of them. "My master was right! The dragons never lie ... and here you are."

"Illium ..." Joryn spoke through intense fear.

The unicorn wasted no time in springing his own weaponry from his sides and aiming his guns right at the creature.

Joryn laughed and patted the unicorn's neck. "Not *every* weapon in Bluepearl, eh?"

Warclaw stopped in his tracks and puzzled over this. "Is this the same unicorn I tore to pieces the last time we met?"

"The same," Joryn answered coldly. "Armed with Deluvian light rays. Now talk. Who is your master, and what is your master's quarrel with us?"

The monstrous creature narrowed his eyes. "I serve the Wanderer of legend. He wants to hurt King Sapros by destroying the ones he loves."

Dismissing as fabrication the monster's claim to serve such a mythical evil as the Wanderer, Joryn stood his ground. "Then I suppose he hasn't heard. I am my father's least favorite son."

"The youngest ones always feel that way," Warclaw countered. "And the youngest sons are always the dearest."

Joryn reached for his sword, then remembered he had none. He whispered to his unicorn. "Illium, can you set for stun?"

Illium gave a nod, and a subtle click could be heard within him as the weapons changed power sources.

"Leave us, now, Warclaw, and we will have mercy on you."

"What good is your mercy compared to my master's wrath? Did you not see that he has the power to teleport his minions here? Imagine what else such power can do. He is the most terrible wizard in all of Nod. I cannot return without your head."

The monster moved forward, and Illium opened fire.

Without warning, from within the chasms all around them, a swarm of the strange winged dragon men they had seen in Bluepearl flew to Warclaw's defense with shields and swords drawn, blocking the stun beams just in time to prevent them from hitting their target.

Warclaw took advantage of the shock he saw painted on Joryn and Illium's faces to lash out with one of his giant claws and knock them aside like insects.

They were airborne for only a moment, but it seemed an eternity, as they wondered whether they would land high or fall to their deaths in one of the chasms. Ultimately, luck was on their side, as they hit the top of a pathway hard.

Illium's machinery whirred and clanked miserably as he got to his feet. His guns had automatically retracted when he had gone into the air. The hatches were bent. He couldn't get them back out. "We have a problem."

"What do you mean, Illium?"

Just then, the colossal crab man leapt at them, knocking Joryn aside. He kicked Illium off of his feet and began hammering at the unicorn's prosthetics with both of his claws, rending metal and smashing gears.

Joryn forced himself back up and ran at Warclaw. "No! I won't let you hurt him!"

"Too late for that, little bug. He's already dead." Warclaw kicked the unicorn over the side of the chasm. They heard a loud crash as Illium's broken cybernetic body hit a ledge below.

"Monster!" Joryn ran at Warclaw, and the villain laughed as though it were a jest.

"Now for that foolish head of yours." Warclaw opened and closed his pincers with delight, then lowered them to deal a fatal blow.

It was then, and without any explanation, that the dragon men turned on Warclaw. They surrounded him in the air, not letting him get his pincers to the young human at all. He swatted at them, never making contact, as they led him to the opposite chasm. Before Warclaw knew what was happening, he was losing his footing and flailing in the air. The monster screamed as he fell over backwards into the abyss.

Joryn did not stop to ask after the motives of the dragon men. He went immediately to the edge of the chasm where

Illium had fallen and found the broken unicorn lying on a narrow ledge fifteen feet below. He turned to the dragon men then. "Please; I can't save him alone. Help me lift him out of there."

The dragon men simply stared at him, then passed glances between themselves. One of them finally spoke, "Why should our queen worry over the fate of your steed? It is you who have requested an audience, and it is for you that she waits. If you travel day and night without sleeping, you can make your appointment on foot. I advise you to forget about the unicorn. It would take all the time you have just to get him out of there on your own."

"Then help me," Joryn pleaded.

The dragon men took to the air and headed to the mountains that now dominated the horizon.

"*Please!*" Joryn fell to his knees, suffering a moment of despair. He dragged himself over to the edge and stared down at his brave friend. Without hesitation, he crawled over the edge and began to climb down to him. When he got to the unicorn's side, Joryn saw that he was still breathing. Smoke was issuing forth from some of the damaged areas, and gears were clanking and whirring in a way they never had before. He could not help but despair. There was no one within range who could help them. There were no Deluvian scientists to repair Illium. They had traveled too far.

Illium was lost.

Joryn buried his head in the creature's white fur and began to sob like a child.

Illium did not have the strength to lift his head, but he spoke, "Do not lose hope, my prince. You may still make it on time, as the creatures told you. You will not have the luxury of sleep, but it is possible. You will have to leave me behind, and you *must*. The fate of the border cities rests with your success in the city of the dragons."

The prince composed himself and wiped the tears from his eyes. "I can't do it, Illium. I can't leave you here to die."

"You have no choice." Illium coughed. "Go now. Rescue Galen. Bargain for the salvation of Bluepearl and the other cities." The unicorn's eyes smiled. "I know that you can do this. You have always had such gifts. It has truly been an honor to know you."

"You're my best friend, Illium. It's been *more* than an honor for me." He stood with unyielding determination.

"Now shut up and try to think of a way to get us *both* out of here."

The unicorn would almost certainly have argued, if he had not lost consciousness at that very moment.

Joryn surveyed their surroundings. He could easily climb out of the chasm, just as he'd climbed down into it, but Illium was much too heavy for him to carry. He looked down into the darkness of the cold abyss. He could climb down and look for secret tunnels, maybe find a friendly stranger dwelling in the shadows, but the risk outweighed the slim chances of success. What good would it do them if he got himself killed in the process?

After nearly an hour of solid thinking, Joryn slumped beside his friend, making certain that the unicorn was still breathing. He reached out and stroked Illium's mane. "Forgive me, Illium. I can't get you out of here." He leaned over tearfully and kissed his dear friend on the cheek. "And I can't leave you here alone. If you can hear me, this is my plan. The only course left to us is to pray. I will pray for a rescue. And I will not move until it comes. Join me now, if you can."

Joryn bowed his head and prayed. He prayed more fervently than he had ever done before, to whatever god would listen.

He was interrupted by something falling against his head. Joryn opened his eyes and saw that someone had tossed down the end of a very long rope. He stood, shocked by the swiftness with which his prayer had been answered. He looked up and saw a man in a hooded cloak.

"Take the rope, and tie it like a harness around your friend," the man shouted down in a soothing, helpful voice.

"But that's not going to work," Joryn shouted back. "He's not an ordinary unicorn. He's too heavy, and the broken metal of his body may cut through the rope."

There was a smile in the man's voice, "Not this rope, Joryn. Do as I have said, and I will lift him up."

"You'll lift him by yourself?"

"Stranger things have happened, young prince. Now do as I have said."

Deciding that he had nothing to lose for trying, Joryn did as the man said, tying Illium snugly around all of his legs, so that if this man were as strong as he believed himself to be, there would be as little discomfort to the unicorn as possible, as his weight would be evenly distributed. "I've done as you told me," Joryn shouted up.

"Good." The man took his end of the rope and walked back out of sight. Joryn watched as the slack went taut, then with wonder as Illium began to rise.

The man lifted Illium all the way to the top and over the edge of the cliff from which he'd fallen.

Joryn stood on the ledge below, his mouth gaping in astonishment.

The man looked over the edge once more. "Were you going to join us?" He laughed warmly and backed away.

Joryn scaled the rocky wall in no time and rose out of the chasm to find yet another miraculous sight. "Illium!"

The unicorn turned, completely repaired, as if the second encounter with Warclaw had never occurred. "My prince. It seems your plan has worked." The unicorn whinnied with delight and trotted over to Joryn.

Joryn hugged his neck and spoke to the man in awe, "Thank you, sir. Thank you." He studied Illium's shining prosthetics then spoke to the man through joyous laughter, "It's a wonder with such power that you couldn't have made him whole again."

The man shrugged with a smile. "That wasn't your heart's prayer. You wanted him out and to survive. He could do that just as well with mechanical legs as with organic."

Joryn was disturbed. "You heard my prayer?"

"It was relayed to me. I don't listen to prayers, only to the Power that does."

"Is that how you know my name?"

"I have been following you a while now."

"How long?"

"Just a little over twenty years."

Joryn tried to place the man by his voice, wondering now if this was some old friend or member of his father's court, but nothing about the man's shrouded countenance seemed familiar.

The man smiled again. "I have something for you."

"More than what you've already given me?" Joryn looked to Illium, then back to the stranger. "I could never ask for more."

"That is why these things shall be yours." The man pulled a shining gold and silver sword, along with a matching shield, from within his tattered robe. "Come and take these things, as a favor to me, if you will."

Joryn's eyes went wide in disbelief, as he recognized the sign of Libran on the gifts. "Sir, if I had not seen such wonders already in your presence, I wouldn't believe my eyes. It seems you hold the Sword of Libran!"

"Not for long," said the man. "These are meant for you. You cannot go on unarmed."

Joryn walked towards the man and reached out to take the gifts. To his amazement, the sword and shield transformed dramatically upon being transferred from the stranger's hands to his. The brilliant gold and silver luminescence of the blade and outer side of the shield turned pitch black, with the writing etched into them, ancient lettering that Joryn could not decipher, shining bright white along the blade and the border of the shield in contrast. The underside of the shield, and the hilt of the sword remained golden, but the otherworldly brightness immediately faded from their now more worldly gleam. It was as if the weapons had not simply been delivered from one man to another, but from one state of being into another as well; from the realm of the divine into the world of mortals.

Amidst his wonder, there seemed no appropriate response, no adequate expression of gratitude for the gifts.

"Not that I'm displeased by any means, but would a *simple* sword and shield not do?" He laughed.

"Not for my champion, Joryn."

"Your champion?" He continued to laugh, nervously. "You flatter me, sir. I'm no hero." He held the sword aloft, admiring the way it glimmered in the sunlight. "Only one hero has ever carried the Sword and Shield of Libran. The legends say when he was ready to go to sleep with his ancestors, he handed them back to him, to Libran, and they have not been seen in Nod since. That was supposed to have happened three thousand years ago."

"Yes" the stranger confirmed. "The legends are true. He was a noble hero and a dear friend. I was sad the day he went Home. And I have carried the Sword and Shield ever since, waiting for a worthy heir to their legacy."

Joryn's eyes again went wide with understanding. Beside him, Illium's horn began to glow gold with excitement at the full comprehension of the power now in their midst.

Overwhelmed by the realization, Joryn found himself struggling to put his thoughts to words. "You're …?"

The smile in the man's voice was undeniable, as he answered the unfinished question. "I am Libran." He threw back his hood to reveal a face white as ivory, golden hair that glowed like the Sword had done in his hands, and golden eyes to match. He stepped out of his robe, revealing his great, white, feathered wings. He looked very similar to the men of the sky kingdom of Celestia, save for his great size and otherworldly glow.

Joryn fell to his knees. "Libran! God of Balance …"

"Don't bow down to me, Joryn," Libran said. "I have never called myself a god. Balance, however, has always been my aim."

Joryn stood, puzzled by the ethereal being's words.

"You have shown me what I knew you would, and now you have my mark." Libran nodded to the Sword and Shield. "This will grant you authority in high places. It pleased me to see you ask Illium not to kill Warclaw, when that would have been so easy. You would not have been where you were when I rescued you, if you had not valued life as much as I do. While you would have shed the blood of the dragons in Bluepearl, you knew that nothing your sword could have done would have killed a single one. You won the day with words, as only a true hero could. Keep these values in your heart forevermore, and I will stand by you, even if you fail. Value life. Defend the defenseless. And pray not to me, but to the Power that created Nod and every world. This is the Power that I serve, and your prayers will be relayed to me, when they are sincere.

"Go now to Din, and do what you can for Galen and the border cities. All that you need is now in your possession."

Libran returned to his tattered robe and hood, and he walked into the very ether, vanishing from sight.

Joryn and Illium were both weeping silently at the beauty of the miracle they had just witnessed. It took several long moments before they felt able to speak or to move, out of reverence for the words of Libran.

CHAPTER 7:

LAST STAND IN THE CITY OF DIN

J ORYN AND ILLIUM TRAVELED WITH ALL SPEED, resting only when they absolutely had to. By the time they entered the mountain range itself, the journey upwards was no more difficult for Illium's tireless mechanical legs. They traveled the mountain paths, encountering no living thing, until they reached the city of Din, two days after their encounter with Libran.

Joryn was awestruck. "Illium, it's incredible!" He could not stop gawking at the immense size of the structures, the pillars and art, the architecture that surrounded them. He was cautious as they stopped at the towering gate at the city wall. They saw dragons flying to and fro in the air, filling the sky like birds, going about their daily business. Joryn felt like an insect. He forced himself to take his gaze from the sky and stare directly at the immense gate before him. "I guess ... do we knock?"

"Good question." The unicorn laughed. "I don't suppose that such a tiny knock on such a titanic gate would be heard by the terrible lizards themselves."

Joryn nodded thoughtfully. "I suppose we could just wait." He patted the unicorn's neck. "But not for long. If I were in your place, I'd be getting ready to kick the door in with those legs of yours."

The unicorn joined the young man in giddy laughter that seemed misplaced, considering the gravity of their situation, but was just the cure to the tension they both felt.

Just then, and without preamble, the gates swung back, and the grandeur they had seen thus far was swept away in comparison to what lay within the city walls. It was a city of towers; a city for winged titans. While some of the massive edifices were built with gigantic stones, some carved into the very mountains themselves, others, indeed the grandest of them all, were constituted purely of crystal and shimmered in the sunlight, their shining prismatic walls and spires refracting the light that passed through them and bathing the whole of the city in a glorious multihued radiance.

Barely able to contain his wonder, Joryn forced himself to remain at the ready. "Do you think they plan to kill us?"

Illium snorted. "Does it matter?"

"No," Joryn answered with total resolve. "We've come this far. Let's see it through."

"Well said." Illium moved ahead, making his way along the golden roads that spread out before them as wide as the open fields he'd been reared in.

After another hour of walking, they found their way to the queen's palace. It had not been hard to identify among the rest of the towering monoliths of the dragons' city. The palace was narrow and tall, like a great needle piercing the very sky. The sun behind it presented the illusion of actually holding the palace aloft. As with the magnificent towers they had seen before, the walls were mostly crystal; every color the human eye could see glistening forth where the light caressed it. This was not the palace of a monster, as Joryn had envisioned it. Rather, this was perhaps the most beautifully crafted structure he had ever seen.

Joryn's reverie was broken, as a familiar dragon landed before him, causing the earth to thunder beneath his feet. Many other dragons landed behind the general as well. "You made it. How you made it, and whether or not you have done a wise thing by keeping your word, is really beside the point. I will acknowledge that I respect you for your strength." Zaur eyed the unicorn. "Before the queen ends your life, I hope that time will permit me to ask certain questions about how you *both* survived." Turning his attention back to the prince and lowering a wing to the ground like a ramp, he beseeched them, "Now climb onto my back. We must enter the palace, and it was not designed for humans or unicorns. One must have wings to get from level to level."

Joryn and Illium exchanged a glance. Joryn patted the unicorn, and Illium accepted the invitation by walking up the dragon's wing and taking a place on his back, bracing himself. Joryn remained astride Illium's saddle, too uncertain of his own footing on the dragon's back to risk a dismount.

The dragon grinned. "Of course, great size has its merits as well." He flapped his wings and took to the air, soaring through the gates of the palace high above the ground. Zaur took them through the corridors and up through the many levels of the glimmering palace, until they came to an arena, small by the measurements of a dragon, but overwhelming in size to creatures as tiny as Joryn and Illium. Zaur let them off in the middle of the arena, then flew up to take a seat on a terrace above them. "And now you may have your parley."

When Zaur simply sat, staring at them expectantly for several minutes, Joryn nervously asked, "Is the queen on her way?"

"No *human* sees the queen. She would not lower herself. I shall speak on her behalf." Smoke billowed from Zaur's nostrils, making Joryn think of a predator whose mouth was watering in anticipation of the kill.

Joryn slid off of Illium's back and stood beside him. "Then let us begin. I seek a lasting peace between humans and dragons. I seek an end to the hostilities that have been visited on our cities for so long." He paused. "I seek the release of Galen, son of Lord Pleidies."

Zaur spoke in a mocking tone. "These are decisions only the queen can make. Your people are offensive and weak. I can make no proclamation in her stead that you would find favorable."

"Then how are we to come to any settlement? I must speak with the queen ..." Joryn stopped himself, remembering what his brother Kail had taught him about diplomacy. "I *humbly* request an audience with the queen. If my scent or the sight of me is offensive to her, then I would cover myself, so as not to offend her. If only the queen has the wisdom and the authority to make decisions of this magnitude, then I see no other way."

The dragon responded nonchalantly. "I seem to recall promising you little hope, if not death, upon entering our city. No human has come here and left with his breath still in him as long as I have lived."

"You offered me no encouragement; it is true. If I must die, I will have died to save my people. I will meet my ancestors with dignity."

Zaur smiled. "You *may* yet live, little princeling. However, surely *someone* must die." He snapped his fingers, and two of the mysterious dragon men walked in, pulling aside a curtain to Zaur's right.

"Galen!" Joryn moved forward at the sight of his heart's desire.

The dragon men checked the chains that bound the young man's wrists and ankles to the wall, then they removed the gag from his mouth.

Galen shouted out instantly, "Joryn! Are you *crazy*? What in the moons possessed you to come here?" A joyful tear and a smile forced their way onto the young man's face, in spite of his protest.

Joryn smiled up at him. "You needed rescuing."

Galen rolled his eyes and regarded the chains that held him. "My hero."

Joryn shrugged. "It's a work in progress."

"Enough," Zaur roared. "Bring him in."

The dragon men flew off and came back with one of their own in chains. They set him down in the arena with Joryn and Illium, unshackling him. Joryn noticed this dragon man had weights pierced into his wings. The other dragon men flew back to take their positions on either side of Galen.

"What is this?" Joryn asked.

"This is Kh'A, a rebellious slave. And *this* is the choice before you, young human. Kh'A will be given a weapon with which to defend himself. I warn you that he nearly killed a *dragon* before we locked him away. It seems he doesn't hold with our policies on the treatment of his kind. I am giving you a chance to fight him out of fairness. *No* human can kill a dragon, after all. This creature is closer to your own kind in stature, and his wings no longer fly."

"I did not come here to do battle—"

"But *didn't* you? Surely you knew that only blood would win this day, and surely you craved it as well, *human*. These are the queen's terms. The fight is to the death. If Kh'A kills you, then our peace is broken immediately. We will invade and raze twice as many human cities as we would have otherwise done this year." He eyed Illium. "As for Illium, it has been too long since any in Din have tasted the succulent flavor of unicorn meat." Looking back to Joryn, he went on, "However, if you kill Kh'A, we will release this *other* human to you. You will be given an hour to try and escape. After this, all dragons will be permitted to hunt you with orders to incinerate on sight.

"So you have but this one slim hope, and it hinges all on whether you can best this slave in combat."

Joryn was deeply forlorn, and his posture did nothing to hide it.

The dragon seemed pleased. "Or … you could walk away, right now. Leave us the unicorn and the human filth already in captivity. They will die, but you will live. I will allow you safe passage all the way on your journey, and you will be able to tell your people of any weaknesses you have seen in our lands, you will be able to warn them of our intent and perhaps even live to see us defeated and your friends avenged. We offer you this second hope out of respect for your courage."

Roused to anger by the offer, Joryn drew his magnificent, glistening sword. "To reward courage, you offer a coward's bargain. I will *not* turn away from the path I have followed. I will not turn my back on my friends to save myself."

The dragon snapped his fingers, and the two dragon men flew overhead and dropped a sword and shield down to Kh'A.

The flightless dragon man regarded the weapons and the man before him. He nodded to Joryn, communicating his respect for the young human. He knelt down and retrieved the sword and shield.

Joryn regarded the dragon man he'd been asked to kill. The creature's only crime was rebelling against slavery. Joryn had no quarrel with him. He looked up at Galen, taking in the young man's beauty perhaps for the final time. He looked to General Zaur, as he threw the mighty Sword of Libran to the side and stood defenseless. "And I will *not* kill one innocent creature in order to save another. I didn't come here to fight. I came here to *reason*. Before you kill me, I remind you that it was parley with your *queen* that was promised me. I traveled five days to have her ear; not to shed blood, but to *prevent* bloodshed." A tremor found its way into his voice, as Illium encouraged him to continue with a sure nod. "Please, if only the queen would hear what I have to say ..."

"And so she has," a melodious voice answered from above.

Zaur backed up and bowed low, as the queen flew down from the heights of the palace.

The dragon men knelt down.

Illium knelt down.

Even Kh'A, who did not accept his place as a slave, lowered his head respectfully.

Joryn looked around him and followed Illium's lead.

Zaur announced the new arrival, "All kneel in the presence of Shaakkanaah, Queen of the Dragons."

The queen landed in a great throne on the opposite side of the arena from General Zaur. She studied Kh'A, who still stood. Flame licked the sides of her jaws, causing the jewels that adorned her pink and violet scales to shine with the promise of retribution.

Kh'A kneeled.

"Rise," Shaakkanaah said simply, and all obeyed. She looked to Joryn. "I would like to tell you a story, young human."

Joryn noted that when she'd named his species, a new respect seemed to resonate within the word.

"You have earned an understanding of what has gone before, so that you will understand the decision I must come to ... and have already made." She regarded him silently, waiting for a response.

At last, trying to imagine what his brother Kail would have done in this situation, Joryn decided to answer very simply, with a nod and a slight bow of his shoulders. "Queen Shaakkanaah, it is my honor to listen."

"Indeed." She regarded the prince approvingly then went ahead with her speech. "Human kind has inhabited the land of Nod for thousands of years. However, dragon kind has inhabited Nod for *millions*. Our history is so far reaching that none of us know the tales of every era. It is known to all dragons only that Nod was created *for* us, as a sanctuary. The world we came from had been given over to a new age. It had been promised by the One to humans, who would in time replace us as its rulers.

"We ruled Nod, marveling at its wonders, its beauty, and its infinite nature for more years than humans have even yet existed. The Outer World was yours. Nod was ours. There was peace.

"Then, not very long ago by *our* reckoning, a human couple was banished to Nod. The best of dragons had come here as a reward, but these humans came here in disgrace, as criminals, unable to remain with their own kind. With these two humans came the 'gods,' as you now call them, and with the 'gods' came war.

"Their descendants grew quite numerous and, once the humans' little empire had been established, war among the various peoples of Nod became commonplace. The dragons decided to show them all who was the master of warfare. We would test the humans; these tiny creatures who the One had designed to rule—to *replace* us—in the Outer World. These creatures who had brought nothing but evil to our once wholly peaceful land. We began the tradition, every three human kings, that you have come this day to protest."

The queen smiled, gazing intensely at Joryn.

He blanched, but stood firm, eyeing Illium beside him.

"Every time we invaded your cities, we waited, *hoped*, for one of your number to come to us and prove your race worthy of our consideration. There were many who challenged us. They all failed the tests. The only one, before you, who made it to this chamber, I personally incinerated, when he chose to abandon his love. She was chained to that very wall, where Galen is, two thousand years ago. I killed her next; for what use were any humans if this man had represented their best?

"Now *you* have come before us. And we have tested you harshly." She looked to Galen, though still speaking to Joryn. "Your heart's desire was stolen and taken to the land of your enemies." Her gaze moved back to Joryn. "Most of the humans we have tested thus failed immediately, and our razing of the cities went ahead. They accepted that their true love was lost. They fell to despair and risked nothing. *You* snuck off in the night, risking your father's wrath, risking your very life, to come after this one special person. Then you found yourself in Bluepearl.

"Few humans chose to follow their heart's desire at all, but all who did eventually met the dragons in some city at the border. None of these cities still stand, mind you, because we destroyed them in the end. Most were destroyed on the very day our chosen human arrived, because he or she saw the carnage or the dragons in flight and fled from the city, either intending to leave the city to its fate while they pursued their love, or turning back and accepting defeat. *You* thought defeat was eminent in Bluepearl, but you never surrendered hope. *You* faced General Zaur and earned a brief reprieve for the city, not with violence, but with words."

She eyed Illium. "Your companion was fatally wounded along the way, and none would help you to save him. What would you do? Others in your position had chosen to leave their friends to die, though it pained them greatly to do so. They were so intent on their personal quest, that nothing else was as important. Our warriors killed them on the road. They never even reached this city. *You* found yourself in a hopeless situation and turned your back not on your friend or your beloved, but on the situation itself, surrendering to a higher power and finding new pathways where none had previously existed.

"As for the final tests, I already told you of the one man who made it that far before you and of his failure. We had hopes. In the end, his heart unfortunately failed him. Do not think us liars. It was Zaur alone who made you that same guarantee of freedom should you choose to walk away. I made no such promise, and the rule of the queen is supreme in the land of dragons.

"So it was, in this final test, *you* did not fail at all. You once again refused to abandon your friend or your beloved. And, most impressive of all, you refused to take the life of Kh'A in order to save your beloved and your steed." She nodded towards the Sword, as it lay on the ground nearby. "Surely, any who would throw down the Sword of Libran rather than use it to strike down another living creature, are the very ones who are worthy to wield it."

Her voice sounded self-satisfied, as she noted the look of surprise in the young prince's expression. "Yes, I know the Sword of Libran. I have seen it before, in my looking globes, in the time when another hero carried it always at his side. I often wondered what would have happened if Libran's champion had been alive during one of the generations in which we performed our tests. Though the other so-called 'gods' are putrid to us, the dragons of Din have the highest respect for the being known as Libran. And it seems I have, after all these millennia, finally found my answer, and humans have found their champion."

Joryn was uncomfortable with so much being placed on his shoulders. "I haven't done anything so great as you make it sound. I …"

"You have saved humanity. You have proved that there is genuine value within their race. Your modesty really shouldn't surprise me, and yet it does. So make your request to me now. As the queen of all dragons, I will grant right now any request made to me by the only human in all of history ever to pass the dragons' tests."

Joryn was elated, terrified, and feeling somewhat faint. He looked to Illium, then to Galen on the wall.

Illium gave him an encouraging gaze with those smiling eyes of his.

Galen smirked, as if holding back a laugh, but a tear had rolled down his cheek, and the chains had prevented him from stopping it. He'd been powerfully moved by the dragon's tale but didn't seem to want it to show.

Joryn looked to the slave he'd chosen not to kill, then to Queen Shaakkanaah. "What becomes of Kh'A?"

"He dies," she said simply. "His use has ended, for he is a rebellious slave."

Joryn kneeled before the great dragon. "Queen Shaakkanaah, as the son of King Sapros, emperor of the human territories of Nod, I come before you to request an end to hostilities between the dragons and the humans of Nod. I request the release of my beloved Galen." He paused and took a breath, bracing himself. "And I request the release of Kh'A from all charges and from his bonds."

The dragon queen reared up, surprised. Joryn noted a similar look of shock on the faces of all in the room, save Illium. Illium rarely seemed genuinely surprised by anything.

"My queen ..." Zaur began, frightened of her wrath.

"Silence, General." Queen Shaakkanaah composed herself quickly. "I have said that I would grant the requests of Prince Joryn, son of King Sapros of the human empire. And so I shall." She glared at the young prince. "However, this last request is not a welcome one. You have taken a great risk in making it, which seems to be a simple fact of your character. Freeing a rebellious slave is the most dangerous thing any ruler can do." She stared the young prince down, before continuing. "But so is breaking her word. There shall be peace between the dragons and the humans, as long as Joryn, son of Sapros, draws breath, and after, so long as the humans do not break the truce themselves."

She looked to the wall where the other young human stood chained. "Galen, son of Pleidies, shall be released from his bonds."

Her eyes narrowed, as she looked to her slave. "And Kh'A, though I say it with misgivings, shall become the first of his species to be set free, provided that he leaves Din immediately and never returns; for to do so would mark him for immediate death."

Kh'A's eyes glistened with joy as he met the eyes of Joryn. However, he knew that when the queen said *immediately*, she meant nothing less, and he did not want to tempt fate at that particular moment even by offering his thanks. He turned without a word and left the room.

The other dragon men, after releasing Galen, followed Kh'A and removed the weights from his wings.

"His entire *species* is enslaved here?" Joryn asked incredulously.

The queen regarded him with eyes narrowed to slits, smoke rising from her snout menacingly. "Choose your battles carefully, young hero. You have won a great day for your people, and it had everything to do with humans. What you speak of now is a matter only involving the dragons of Nod. Do not try my patience in matters that need not concern you."

Accepting that, for the time, he had won peace and freedom for at least one of the peoples of Nod, Joryn chose to accept his victory and leave in the queen's good graces; though the lesson did not escape him that there would remain creatures in Nod in need of a hero; the dragon men likely being just the beginning. Joryn found he hated the balancing act that was politics but felt that he might yet become very good at it.

The queen spread her wings, and her mood lifted. "You are audacious, and you dare to vex me, but you are very wise. Libran chose you well. I look forward to seeing what you become." She lifted into the air. "You have my permission to visit the dragons whenever it pleases you to do so. In fact, consider it an invitation, my very *interesting* young human." She flew to the highest heights of the palace, and all below watched in awe as she departed; not least of all General Zaur, who'd thought this day would never come.

CHAPTER 8:

THE PEACE-BRINGER

As ILLIUM CARRIED JORYN AND GALEN FROM the city of the dragons, Galen rested his head on Joryn's shoulder. "I think I love you," he said simply.

Joryn laughed. "I think I already knew that."

"Yes, but I didn't know how *much* you loved *me*. You risked ..." He couldn't even put the full weight of his gratitude into words. How could he *ever* find the words? He decided to change the subject, noticing the weapon clipped to Illium's side. "And is that *really* the Sword of Libran? From the god *himself?* You have to tell me the story! I want to know about everything you went through."

"And I want to know all about *your* adventures as a prisoner of the dragons."

Galen laughed. "I wouldn't exactly call it an *adventure*. I was tied up mostly. But still, I suppose it was an experience worth telling about."

Joryn smiled, happier than he'd felt in all the time since he'd first met Galen. "It is a long journey back to the palace."

"Good," Galen said, surprising Joryn with his sincerity. "I'm in no hurry to be flown back to the Whispering Plains. Besides, home's much too far away from my heart."

Joryn only smiled in reply.

As the three friends traveled, they shared many stories.

Word of Joryn's successful negotiations with the dragons reached his father's palace before they did. Joryn and Illium received a hero's welcome and were pressed to tell the tale of their adventure so many times that it became almost a task for young Joryn.

When Lord Pleidies prepared once more to depart for the Whispering Plains, Joryn made a point not to be late to see Galen off. He ran to him at the ramp of the flying craft that was ready to take all the dignitaries home. They took hold of each other, looking into each other's eyes and silently coming to a decision about the nature of their relationship. Joryn grinned, and Galen had only just begun to smile back, when Joryn leaned in and kissed him, deeply, for all the world to see. There would be no more secrets, no more pretending that what they had found in each other was anything less than what it truly was. The kiss lingered, unencumbered by the finite nature of the time that remained to them, and they lived in the moment, holding the embrace, for as long as time allowed.

That evening, long after Galen had departed for the Whispering Plains, Prince Kail found his youngest brother once again on the ledge outside of the palace, gazing across the Celestine Sea as the sun set on the horizon, seeming to sink into the endless waters, bringing yet another day to its end. "So, I see you've managed to escape from your princely duties once again."

Joryn turned with a wry grin. "You're joking, I hope."

Kail laughed. "Of course. I'd say you've more than done your fair share of 'duty' in the past several weeks."

Joryn turned his gaze back on the sunset. "It's sort of hard to accept."

"What is?"

"All of it. Just days ago, I was a normal prince, with a normal, albeit vastly ancient, unicorn, and my father held me in utter contempt. Today, I'm a hero, with the world's only bionic unicorn for a companion, the Sword of Libran at my side, and my father's … I wouldn't call it respect."

"Fear." Kail sounded grim.

"Yes. I think he's afraid of me now." He unsheathed the Sword of Libran and studied it in the fading sunlight. "I think he's afraid of this."

"It is magnificent, isn't it?"

"It is." Joryn returned the blade to the scabbard at his belt and turned away from his brother, as an unexpected tear escaped his eye.

"Is it that bad, Little Brother?"

"No. Just … a change."

"For the better I'd say. Your legend is already forever. Joryn the Peace-Bringer."

"That's just it though, Kail. I suspect the 'legend' has only just begun. I can't see a being such as Libran bestowing the lost treasure of his Sword and Shield upon me for a single task. Not after three thousand years of waiting. Think of the hero who carried them before. No." He nodded to the horizon. "That sunset does not mark the end of just another day. It marks the end of my life."

Concerned, Kail stood close beside his brother and studied his deadly serious expression. "What are you saying?"

Joryn laughed at his brother's worry and wiped the tears from his cheeks with a forced smile, trying to show his brother that he hadn't meant a literal or terrible thing by his words. "All I'm saying is that the boy I was has died. Even the man I was on the path to becoming. I'm someone else now. Renewed and recreated no less than noble Illium. I know in my heart that I will be used until I die in the service of our world." He clutched the hilt of the Sword at his side. "From this day forth, my life belongs to Nod."

The saga of *The Sword of Libran* will continue,

with Book II:

All for the Blood of Nightstorm

Selections from Parakletos'
Annals of Nod

Approximately 66,032,113 Years Before the Twelve (BT)

The universe of Nod is brought into being.

The dragons from the Outer World arrive and take their place as Nod's dominant species, founding the city of Din, on the continent of Ana Eridu.

32,181,785 BT

(Month 1: Day 4) The three great unicorn plains of Ana Eridu unite to form the kingdom of Elysium, a three-state monarchy ruled by their chosen leader, King Nandor.

Year 1 of the Twelve (YT)

The first humans arrive in Nod, from the Outer World, along with the powerful immortal beings known commonly as the Twelve Great Gods of Nod.

1,268 YT

(Month 7: Day 24) The city of Bluepearl is founded, when the hero Lander brings his nomadic human tribe, the People of Stone Foot, a magical blue pearl thought to be a fallen piece of the blue moon Cerulea. As it was believed, the magic pearl grants his people perennially fertile soil and previously unknown prosperity, bringing an end to generations of itinerancy.

1,512 YT

(Month 9: Day 12) The Wanderer emerges as a powerful sorcerer and enemy of Nod's humans, when he engulfs the village of Skaaldu in a mystic fire that cannot be extinguished until the last building is burnt to ash.

1,628 YT

(Month 2: Day 20) The human luminary, Orie I, founds the Kingdom of Nod, a city kingdom named after the universe itself. Orie I declares himself the city's king, naming his son, Orie II, as his heir apparent, intending to establish a dynastic monarchy for generations to come.

1,846 YT

(Month 10: Day 4) The Sentinel Knights and the Wizards Wyrloq work together to bind the Wanderer in a mystical stasis prison, in a cavern deep beneath the inhospitable terrain of Spike Island, intending to leave him imprisoned there for all time.

2,064 YT

(Month 8: Day 15) The city of Bluepearl is annexed by the Kingdom of Nod, by order of King Joseph.

2,464 YT

(Month 5: Day 9) Taking advantage of recent wars and forged alliances, King Simon of the Kingdom of Nod establishes an empire that includes a number of weaker kingdoms, whose rulers will henceforth answer to him as their emperor. The empire is called the Empire of Nod, named for its ruling kingdom. The name of the Kingdom of Nod's capital city is changed from the City of Nod to Imperial City.

2,578 YT

(Month 9: Day 27) Queen Shaakkanaah, of the Empire of Dragons, long vexed by the arrogance of the human interlopers, launches her first assault against the Empire of Nod, during the reign of Emperor Rodgerus, the third emperor of Nod.

2,846 YT

(Month 4: Day 2) During the Mystic War's Battle of Spike Island, the Wanderer is released from his ancient stasis prison, unleashing his sinister sorcery on the people of Nod once again.

2,847 YT

(Month 5: Day 21) The god Libran chooses a hero named Bran to represent his interests in the world of Nod, gifting him with weapons that will come to be called the Sword of Libran and the Shield of Libran.

2,865 YT

(Month 2: Day 28) The human, Aero, is born to Bran and Illana.

2,882 YT

(Month 10: Day 12) The Wanderer unleashes the horrors of the Darkening Scourge on the world of Nod, even as he engages Aero in battle. Aero reportedly slays the Wanderer in single combat, only to die himself from lethal wounds inflicted upon him during the battle, and the Darkening Scourge begins to spread across the land.

(Month 10: Day 12) Just before his death, Bran returns the Sword and Shield of Libran to their immortal eponym, who holds the arms in trust for a future hero who will be deemed worthy of their legacy. Bran sacrifices his life returning the Darkening Scourge to its eternal prison.

3,940 YT

(Month 5: Day 7) The kingdom of Celestia becomes a part of the Empire of Nod, at the conclusion of the Goodspeed-Starlight Accords, between Emperor Goodspeed of the Empire of Nod and Chief Starlight of the kingdom of Celestia. This is the first time a primarily non-human state is granted membership in the Empire.

4,824 YT

(Month 9: Day 22) The Wanderer emerges from Mount Dread, despite the reports of his death, and announces his return by unleashing his dark sorcery on the kingdom of Ironstryke, in the Empire of Nod. He manages to sink the city into an underground lava pool before anyone realizes the full extent of his power. Warriors from the Imperial Guard and the Celestian Vanguard arrive to aid the survivors, only to have the Wanderer evade capture and launch a new campaign of terror and revenge upon the Empire. Historical accounts remain unclear as to whether this was the same ancient villain allegedly slain by Aero, or another villain altogether.

4,882 YT

(Month 3: Day 10) The unicorn, Illium, is born to Ryjan and Maladine in the Golden Field.

(Month 10: Day 30) During the Battle of Oblivion Rock, the Wanderer is purportedly slain by the renowned hero Palo, who combines sorcery with swordplay to best the villain in a contest of might. As with Aero before him, the wounds he sustains throughout the duel see to it that the victory costs Palo his own life. This is the last reported appearance of the sorcerer known as the Wanderer.

4,982 YT

(Month 4: Day 23) Illium is knighted by King Néos, in the Order of the Golden Field, for his valor during the Alicorn War.

(Month 9: Day 23) The kingdom of Elysium becomes a part of the Empire of Nod, at the conclusion of the Gobil-Néos Accords, between Emperor Gobil of the Empire of Nod and King Néos of the kingdom of Elysium.

5,226 YT

(Month 3: Day 17) The Twelve Tribes of the centaurs become a part of the Empire of Nod, at the conclusion of the Nod-Centaur Accords, between Emperor Robert III of the Empire of Nod and Lord Caluman LXV of the Twelve Tribes.

5,329 YT

(Month 4: Day 2) During the reign of Emperor Morgan, the sixty-third emperor of Nod, the dragons of Din launch their twenty-first assault against the Empire of Nod, led for the first time by the dragon General Zaur.

5,581 YT

(Month 6: Day 15) Sir Illium and Norlan are married.

5,582 YT

(Month 6: Day 16) The unicorn, Charger, is born to Sir Illium and Lady Norlan in the Field of Crystal.

5,792 YT

(Month 3: Day 15) An Imperial colony is founded in the Whispering Plains, under a charter penned by Emperor Edward II of the Empire of Nod, for the purpose of mining the region's rich deposits of ceresia ore.

5,817 YT

(Month 4: Day 25) The human, Sunjac, is born to Governor Bonak and Lady Perriella in the city of Bluepearl.

5,822 YT

(Month 9: Day 5) The human, Prince Sapros, is born to Emperor Barnard and Empress Mideerma at Palace Nod, in Imperial City.

5,830 YT

(Month 12: Day 29) The human, Pleidies, is born to Lord Verdan and Lady Saniru at Ruby Point.

5,844 YT

(Month 1: Day 28) The centaur, Dorran Equus, is born to Rinaulf Equus and Gylanna Equus in the nomadic tribe of Caluman.

(Month 11: Day 16) Prince Sapros and his first wife are married. The bride is granted the title of Princess.

5,847 YT

(Month 5: Day 19) The human, Prince Kail, is born to Prince Sapros and his first wife, the Unnamed Princess, at palace Nod, in Imperial City.

5,849 YT

(Month 12: Day 22) Prince Sapros and Makhaira are married. As a secondary spouse, Makhaira is granted the title of Lady.

5,852 YT

(Month 3: Day 18) The human, Prince Repteré, is born to Prince Sapros and his second wife, Lady Makhaira, at Palace Nod, in Imperial City.

(Month 5: Day 19) Charger becomes the royal steed of Prince Kail, on the prince's fifth birthday.

5,853 YT

(Month 8: Day 14) The human, Princess Willowyll, is born to Prince Sapros and his second wife, Lady Makhaira, at Palace Nod, in Imperial City.

5,854 YT

(Month 1: Day 11) Prince Sapros and Lady Amina are married.

(Month 8: Day 8) Prince Sapros and Lady Leita are married.

(Month 11: Day 10) The human, Prince Dakarai, is born to Prince Sapros and his third wife, Lady Amina, at Palace Nod, in Imperial City.

5,855 YT

(Month 5: Day 11) Pleidies and Galendria are married.

(Month 11: Day 23) The human, Princess Hero, is born to Prince Sapros and his fourth wife, Lady Leita, at Palace Nod, in Imperial City.

5,856 YT

(Month 1: Day 27) Lord Verdan and Lady Saniru are killed by anti-colonial raiders; Pleidies inherits their titles and estates, including the colonial lordship of the Whispering Plains.

(Month 5: Day 4) The human, Prince Mwana, is born to Prince Sapros and his third wife, Lady Amina, at Palace Nod, in Imperial City.

(Month 8: Day 16) Prince Sapros and Lady Riko are married.

5,857 YT

(Month 9: Day 10) The human, Princess Adaeze, is born to Prince Sapros and his third wife, Lady Amina, at Palace Nod, in Imperial City.

(Month 11: Day 30) The human, Kabed, is born in the kingdom of Deluvia.

5,858 YT

(Month 9: Day 5) The human, Prince Dorago, is born to Prince Sapros and his fifth wife, Lady Riko, at Palace Nod, in Imperial City, on Prince Sapros' thirty-sixth birthday.

5,859 YT

(Month 5: Day 20) The noted philosopher Parakletos accepts a position at Palace Nod as tutor to the emperor's grandson, Prince Kail.

(Month 10: Day 15) The human, Princess Enjinia, is born to Prince Sapros and his fifth wife, Lady Riko, at Palace Nod, in Imperial City.

5,860 YT

(Month 4: Day 27) The human, Prince Vail, is born to Prince Sapros and his fourth wife, Lady Leita, at Palace Nod, in Imperial City.

5,861 YT

(Month 1: Day 7) Emperor Barnard of the Empire of Nod dies at the age of one hundred two, having reigned for fifty years. His son, Sapros, is crowned the ninety-fifth king of the Kingdom of Nod and the seventy-fifth emperor of the Empire of Nod. Sapros' first and most beloved wife is crowned empress. Their son, Prince Kail, is named Emperor Sapros' heir apparent.

(Month 11: Day 19) The human, Princess Lily, is born to Emperor Sapros and his fifth wife, Lady Riko, at Palace Nod, in Imperial City.

5,862 YT

(Month 3: Day 13) The human, Prince Joryn, is born to Emperor Sapros and his first wife, the Unnamed Empress, at Palace Nod, in Imperial City.

(Month 8: Day 28) The human, Galen, is born to Lord Pleidies and Lady Galendria in the Imperial colony of the Whispering Plains. Lord Pleidies grants his infant son the entire estate of Ruby Point, from his lands outside of the Plains, in order that his son might begin his life with a title of his own.

5,863 YT

(Month 5: Day 5) The human, Tianna, is born.

(Month 8: Day 6) Tianna is dedicated to the priesthood of Libran.

5,865 YT

(Month 5: Day 18) The official time of Prince Kail's education under Parakletos comes to an end, though the two remain friends, and Parakletos continues to sit on the emperor's Advisory Council.

5,867 YT

(Month 3: Day 13) Sir Illium becomes the royal steed of Prince Joryn, on the prince's fifth birthday.

(Month 3: Day 14) Prince Joryn begins his education under the tutelage of Parakletos.

(Month 7: Day 9) Governor Bonak of the city of Bluepearl dies at the age of seventy-nine, having reigned for sixty-four years. His son, Sunjac, takes his place as the one hundred fifty-second governor of the city of Bluepearl.

5,874 YT

(Month 11: Day 15) The empress of Nod dies at the age of fifty-one. In his grief, Emperor Sapros bans her name from being spoken or written anywhere in the Empire.

5,875 YT

(Month 5: Day 5) On her twelfth birthday, Priestess Tianna begins serving in the Temple of Libran at Palace Nod.

5,877 YT

(Month 1: Day 22) Kabed, now a Deluvian tech wizard, leaves Deluvia and journeys to the Empire of Nod.

(Month 4: Day 13) Kabed meets and befriends Prince Joryn, who convinces Emperor Sapros to take the Deluvian expatriate into the Imperial court as their new head of science. Kabed immediately begins introducing Deluvian technology to the Empire of Nod.

(Month 5: Day 16) The Imperial Guard of Palace Nod begins using Deluvian light guns, in addition to the blades and shields they have used to protect the Empire of Nod for millennia.

(Month 12: Day 28) Dorran Equus is placed in the court of Emperor Sapros by Lord Caluman LXXII, as the Imperial ambassador of the Twelve Tribes of the centaurs.

5,880 YT

(Month 3: Day 12) The official time of Prince Joryn's education under Parakletos comes to an end. As it had been with Prince Kail, Prince Joryn and Parakletos remain friends, and Parakletos continues to sit on the emperor's Advisory Council.

5,881 YT

(Month 3: Day 27) Prince Kail marries Princess Maressah, from the kingdom of Aise; daughter of King Willfriez and Queen Mistrie.

(Month 8: Day 10) Prince Joryn and Lord Galen meet and become friends.

(Month 8: Day 11) Prince Joryn and Lord Galen begin a secret romantic relationship.

5,882 YT

(Month 1: Day 26) Kabed begins working on the prototype for a robotic battle unicorn that he calls a Unitron.

(Month 6: Day 16) Dignitaries from the Whispering Plains, including Lords Pleidies and Lord Galen, arrive at Palace Nod for a three-day visit, in order to attend Charger's tricentennial birthday celebration.

(Month 6: Day 18) Prince Joryn and Sir Illium are attacked by a creature named Warclaw, who claims to be the son of the goddess Cancerelle, and they are soundly defeated. Sir Illium is dismembered by the monster, and Prince Joryn drags him home, where Kabed sets to work trying to save his life.

(Month 6: Day 19) Kabed successfully combines Sir Illium's broken body with the body of his Unitron prototype, saving the ancient unicorn's life and giving him a new set of robotic legs.

(Month 6: Day 19) The dragons of Din, led by General Zaur, attack the Empire of Nod for the twenty-fifth time and take Lord Galen prisoner. Prince Joryn and Sir Illium set out to rescue Lord Galen on their own.

(Month 7: Day 15) The Bluepearl Armistice is declared in the city of Bluepearl, with terms agreed upon verbally, between Prince Joryn of the Empire of Nod and General Zaur of the Empire of Dragons, allowing Prince Joryn one week to reach the city of Din and sue for peace with Queen Shaakkanaah herself before hostilities can resume.

(Month 7: Day 19) The god Libran names Prince Joryn his new champion and successor to Bran, bestowing upon him the legendary Sword of Libran and Shield of Libran, to aid him in his quest.

(Month 7: Day 21) The Shaakkanaah-Joryn Accord is brokered between Prince Joryn of the Empire of Nod and Queen Shaakkanaah of the Empire of Dragons, when the human prince successfully proves the virtues of the human race. In accordance with the terms of the agreement, peace is to stand between the two empires for as long as Prince Joryn draws breath, perhaps even beyond, should the peace accord prove its worth.

ABOUT THE AUTHOR

Glenn Slade Clark, Jr. is the author of seven books, including the novel *Cry, Wolf: Shadow of the Werewolf*, the short fiction anthology *The Great Debate*, the Gothic horror series *The Chronicles of Nightfire, Texas*, and two fantasy series: *Metrognomes* and *The Legends of Nod*. He lives in Dallas, Texas, where he is currently hard at work on the next adventure in *The Legends of Nod*.

www.GlennSladeClarkJr.com

www.ingramcontent.com/pod-product-compliance
Lightning Source LLC
Chambersburg PA
CBHW072031170626
46811CB00008B/3035